D1371739

The
Presidents
of the
United States

The Marshall Cavendish illustrated history of

The
Presidents
of the
United States

Written by
Ruth Oakley

PUBLIC LIBRARY
MAR 1 2 1991
SOUTH BEND, INDIANA

Illustrated by
Steve Lucas and Tim Woodcock-Jones

MARSHALL CAVENDISH
New York · London · Toronto · Sydney

Library Edition Published 1990

© Marshall Cavendish Limited 1990
© DPM Services Limited 1990

Published by Marshall Cavendish Corporation
147, West Merrick Road
Freeport
Long Island
N.Y. 11520

Series created by Graham Beehag Book Design
Designed by Graham Beehag
Produced by DPM Services Limited

All rights reserved. No part of this book may be reproduced or utilized in any form or by any means electronic or mechanical including photocopying, recording, or by any information storage and retrieval system, without permission from the copyright holders.

Library of Congress Cataloging-in-Publication Data

Oakley, Ruth.
  The Marshall Cavendish illustrated history of presidents of the United States / by Ruth Oakley
    p. cm.
  Includes indexes.
  Summary: Places each American preesident in a historical context and discusses his life, with an emphasis on his political activity and presidential term.
    ISBN 1-85435-144-3 (set)
    1. Presidents – United States – Biography – Juvenile literature. 2. United States – Politics and government – Juvenile literature.
[1. Presidents.] I. Title.
E176.8.025 1990
973'.0992 – dc20   89-17283
[B]   CIP
[920]   AC

Printed and bound in the United States of America by Lake Book Manufacturing Inc.

REF j923.173 Oa4p v.1 RBF
Oakley, Ruth.
The Presidents of the
 United States

CONTENTS

Introduction

It is difficult to imagine now how insecure the United States was when George Washington became the first President in 1789. It was not the wealthy and powerful nation that it is today, but a confederation of separate states which had come together to fight Great Britain and gain their independence. Once that battle had been won, the wartime unity of purpose broke down. The economy depended upon agriculture, and there were no reserves in the Treasury. The total population was only four million, of whom seven hundred thousand were slaves. The army and navy were small and weak. Countries such as Britain, France and Spain, powerful and rich, were ruled by monarchs who felt they had the right of conquest over U.S. territory.

After its break from Great Britain, the American nation had been ruled as a confederation. This form of government did not have enough authority to protect the states from harassment by the British and the

Indians on the frontier. American ships were attacked. Individual states quarreled with each other, particularly about taxes.

Yet, by the time James Madison, the fourth president, left office in 1817, the United States was recognized as an independent nation by the major European powers. It had other problems to face, but there was no doubt about its independence.

The men who served the country as the first four presidents — Washington, John Adams, Thomas Jefferson and James Madison, had much in common. They were all of British descent and owned substantial estates, three of them in Virginia. Although Washington did not have much formal education, he had traveled abroad and had a wide variety of experiences. Adams, Jefferson and Madison were all well-educated and intelligent men who were able to respond to the challenges of their age. The new United States was fortunate to be able to call on such honest and capable leaders.

Washington in command on the battlefield at Princeton in 1777.

GEORGE WASHINGTON
(1732-1799)

First President: 1789-1797

"First in war, first in peace, and first in the hearts of his countrymen."
(Henry Lee)

Early life

George Washington was born in 1732 in a simple house at Bridges Creek, Westmoreland County, Virginia, a child of his father's second marriage. His father died when George was eleven. At the age of sixteen he went to live with his half-brother, Lawrence, at his estate, Mount Vernon. Lawrence was kind to him and improved his education. Under his guidance, George acquired the manners and outlook of a country gentleman. In 1751, he took George, by this time a tall, well built young man of great physical strength, to Barbados.

The Country Gentleman

In 1752, at the age of twenty, George unexpectedly inherited the estate following the early death of Lawrence and then of his daughter. Washington's experience of running a large estate and managing men proved valuable to him later, during his time as Commander-in-Chief of the colonial army. He was an enthusiastic farmer, eager to try new ways of increasing yields and improving fertility. When he eventually retired from the presidency in 1796, he

There is no evidence that the famous story of the young George Washington confessing to his father that he cut down a cherry tree is true, but the tale persists in folklore.

found pleasure in introducing new varieties of trees and animals to his estate. One of his great enthusiasms was for hunting, and he was an accomplished horseman. He also enjoyed shooting and fishing.

Military life and marriage

As a lieutenant colonel of the Virginia militia, he fought in the French and Indian Wars. In 1755, he acted as aide to General Braddock, who was advancing on Fort Duquesne, where the French defeated the British. Although four bullets went through his coat and two horses were shot from under him, Washington escaped injury. After the battle, Washington remained in the army. With a force of only three hundred Virginians, he defended the three hundred and fifty mile frontier against Indian raids.

He resigned from the army in 1759 and married Martha Dandridge Custis, a wealthy widow. She was to

9

The British flag is raised at Fort Duquesne in 1758.

remain a constant source of comfort and support to him throughout the Revolutionary War and acted as an elegant and gracious First Lady during his presidency. They had no children of their own, but Washington acted as father to the two surviving children of her previous marriage and as grandfather to their children.

War clouds loom

Washington's enjoyment of life as a farmer, family man and country gentleman was brought to an end for many years by a sequence of events beginning with the Boston Tea Party. At this time, the thirteen states which were later to form the American nation were still colonies ruled and taxed by Great Britain. The colonists objected to paying taxes to a government to which they were not allowed to send representatives and over which they had no influence. When the British government imposed a tax on tea, the simmering resentment boiled over. On December 26,

As a sixteen year old, Washington undertook a wilderness expedition to survey land in the Shenandoah Valley belonging to the Washingtons' wealthy neighbor and relation by marriage, Lord Fairfax. He enjoyed this adventurous experience and learned a great deal about the country and the Indians who lived there.

An English print of 1765 portrays the American colonists as meddling women.

Colonists disguised as Mohawk Indians protest against the tea tax in Boston harbor, 1773.

1773, a party of colonists disguised as Mohawk Indians boarded three vessels in Boston harbor and threw overboard the tea stored in their holds which was worth over $4,500. This act of defiance angered King George III and his Parliament. In March, 1774, the Boston Port Act closed the port of Boston, which meant that the Americans could not trade overseas.

Eventually, anger and defiance against the British led to the First Continental Congress of America in Philadelphia in September, 1774. Washington attended as a delegate from Virginia. Here the Declaration of Rights was adopted. The Congress was not at this stage seeking independence from Britain. It simply wanted a greater recognition of American rights and freedoms. George III and the British Parliament were not prepared to be conciliatory, however, and the situation worsened until war between the two sides became inevitable.

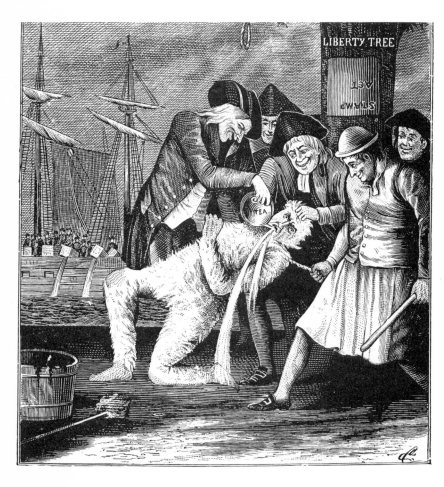

In this British cartoon of 1774 a British tax collector who has been tarred and feathered is being forced to drink British tea underneath a noose. It shows the British anger at the colonists' refusal to accept the authority of George III and Parliament.

Commander-in-Chief

With American victories at the Battles of Lexington and Concord in April, 1775, the war officially began. The British Parliament announced that the colonies were in "open and avowed rebellion." At the Second Continental Congress in 1775, it was unanimously agreed that Washington be appointed as Commander-in-Chief of the Continental Army, a militia made up from conscripts from each of the thirteen states. For the next eight years, until the Peace Treaty signed between Britain and America in 1783, Washington led an "army" which was desperately short of supplies, weapons, ammunition and even shoes. It consisted of untrained men who had only to serve for a year and who would then return to their farms and homes, even if it was the middle of a campaign.

How did such a ragbag bunch ultimately defeat the

Local militia face the British Army at Lexington.

The Battle of Bunker Hill and the burning of Charlestown.

Washington encourages his men in the bleak winter conditions at Valley Forge.

Washington audaciously ferries his forces across the icy Delaware in the stormy night.

might of the highly trained British army? People at all levels of society in America were fired with ideals which had spread across from Europe. They believed passionately in Freedom, Liberty and Independence, and in 1776, the Declaration of Independence was passed. In addition, the United States had only *not to lose* the war: Britain had to win it. The Americans simply had to hold on until Britain became weary of the struggle far from her shores in a country about which little was known by most people of power and influence. Then there was the effect of Washington's leadership. His personal qualities of courage, determination, intelligence and faithfulness to the cause of independence held together the badly-trained and ill-equipped conscript army. Although he was a strict officer, he cared for his men and had compassion for their sufferings.

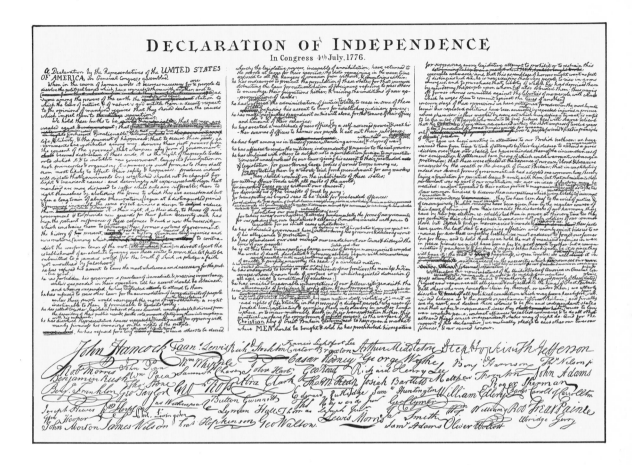

The original Declaration of Independence produced by Thomas Jefferson.

The Declaration of Independence being read to Washington's army in New York, July 9, 1776.

Problems of peace

After the war, Washington was happy to return to Mount Vernon and Martha, but it was not to be for long.

Recognizing that the union between the states was in danger of breaking up, Washington was a prime mover in setting up the Constitutional Convention at Philadelphia in 1787. He presided over this group of revolutionary leaders, who discussed what form of government should be set up and drafted a new constitution. In 1789, Washington was unanimously elected as the first man to hold the office and title of President of the United States. In view of the great respect and admiration felt for him after his unparalleled services to the nation during the Revolutionary War, this choice was not surprising.

The British surrender at Yorktown in 1781.

The Presidency

Washington wrote on taking up the office, "I walk on untrodden ground. There is scarcely any part of my conduct which may not hereafter be drawn into precedent." He realized that any policy he initiated was likely to be a model for future years. He tried not to take power for himself, but to follow the wishes of Congress and his Cabinet.

He was determined to give dignity to the office of President and to make the United States a respected nation around the world. He was very formal in his dress, manner and behavior. He rented the best houses in New York and Philadelphia. Mrs. Washington held a reception every Friday afternoon, at which he often appeared.

During his two terms of office, two main political parties with opposing policies, the Democratic Republicans and the Federalists, began to form. The leader of each party, Thomas Jefferson of the

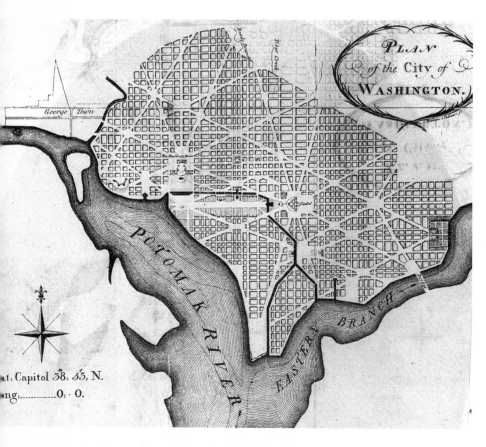

Washington was chosen as the national capital in 1790.

President George
Bush used the same
bible as Washington
for his swearing in
ceremony.

Democratic Republicans and Alexander Hamilton of the Federalists, were in Washington's Cabinet. Although he tried to remain impartial, Washington supported Hamilton, his Secretary of the Treasury, in the establishment of the United States Bank in 1791. Jefferson protested, saying that the act was unconstitutional.

Washington was particularly involved in foreign policy. He recognized that a period of peace was essential to lay secure foundations for the new nation. When war broke out between the British and the French following the French Revolution, Washington insisted that the U.S. should not support either side. He wanted to establish American independence and stability. Jefferson resigned because he believed the United States should honor treaties which she had made with France.

Despite Washington's efforts, friction and rivalry

The stars and stripes of the original Union flag.

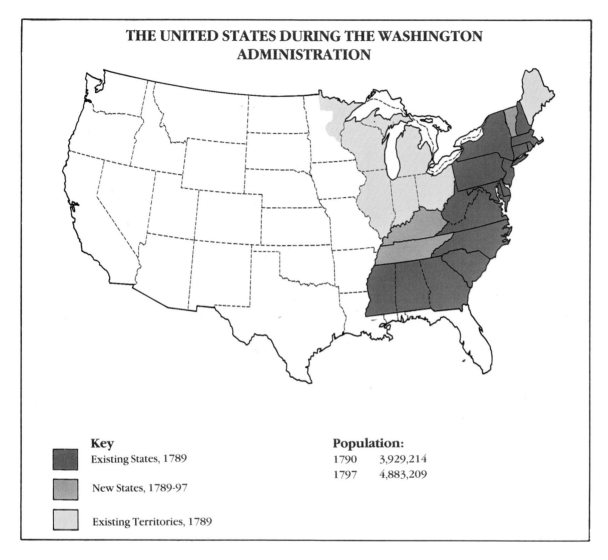

THE UNITED STATES DURING THE WASHINGTON ADMINISTRATION

Key
Existing States, 1789

New States, 1789-97

Existing Territories, 1789

Population:
1790   3,929,214
1797   4,883,209

between the parties increased. During his second term (1792-1797), Washington faced criticism and held less control.

In 1794, there was a rebellion of farmers in western Pennsylvania, who refused to pay tax on whiskey.

When General Braddock was killed in the attempt to take Fort Duquesne from the French, Washington buried his body in the road and ordered carts and horses to trample down and flatten the earth to prevent the Indians from digging up the body and mutilating it.

Although it was quelled without bloodshed and Washington pardoned all prisoners, the incident left bitter feelings. Then, the terms of a treaty with Great Britain regarding American shipping rights caused public indignation. Hamilton resigned following criticism of his handling of the affair.

Retirement

Washington was proud of the honor of being chosen as President. He insisted that, as President of the

Washington loved his home at Mount Vernon in Virginia.

United States, he should be treated with as much respect and ceremony as the monarchs of Europe. However, Washington had not sought the office. After his years as Commander of the Army in the American Revolution, he had looked forward to returning to his

> **Washington's Revolutionary Army was so poorly equipped that few of them had boots. Their path could be traced from their bloodstained footprints. A lead statue of King George III was melted down to make bullets to kill his British soldiers.**

wife and family and to the life of a Virginia gentleman at Mount Vernon. Although he spent much of his life away from home as a soldier, he was a great lover of country life. He had written after the war that he would "be able to view the solitary walk and tread the paths of private life with heartfelt satisfaction."

His retirement came in 1796, when he refused to run for a third term of office and made his Farewell Address. He was called back from retirement briefly when there were fears of a war with France, but the crisis was resolved.

He did not enjoy the peace of Mount Vernon for long. In December, 1799, he caught a cold while riding. It developed into pleurisy, which the doctors were unabe to treat effectively. Weakened by the infection and by being bled to cure it, he died on December 14. His funeral was a simple family affair with a military escort and a salute from local volunteer soldiers. He was buried, as he wished, in the family vault at Mount Vernon, where he rests today with Martha by his side.

> **By the time of his death in 1799, Washington had become one of the greatest landowners in America with over one hundred thousand acres. About two hundred and seventy slaves worked on his plantations. Eventually, he freed them all, as he believed that slavery was wrong in principle, even though his own slaves were well treated.**

The monument to the memory of George Washington in the city which bears his name.

BIOGRAPHY BOX

George Washington

Birthplace	Bridges Creek, Virginia
Date of Birth	February 22, 1732
Education	Public schools
Profession	Planter and soldier
Presidential term	April 30, 1789 to March 4, 1797
Party	No party in his first term and Federalist in his second
Place of death	Mount Vernon, Virginia
Date of death	December 14, 1799
Place of burial	Mount Vernon, Virginia

JOHN ADAMS
(1735-1826)

Second President: 1797-1801

John Adams

Family background

The ancestors of John Adams emigrated to Massachusetts from England in about 1636. His father was a farmer and shoemaker in the town now called Quincy. John attended Harvard College, where he came third in his class for scholastic ability. When he left college, he decided not to become a minister, which was the career his family wanted for him. He felt he could not accept all the beliefs of the Church. Instead, he became a schoolteacher and later was a very successful lawyer.

He married Abigail Smith, the daughter of a Congregational minister. Although she suffered from poor health, she was cheerful and popular. They had a happy family life with a daughter and three sons, one of whom also became President.

His contribution to America's independence and constitution

John Adams had undertaken several diplomatic missions for the United States before he became President in 1797. He visited France and Holland as a government representative. He persuaded the French

Adams showed courage and honesty when he represented the British soldiers accused of the "Boston Massacre." British troops stationed in the port of Boston were much disliked. They were often the target of insult and abuse from the townspeople. On the night of March 5, 1770, the ill-feeling exploded into violence when a group of youths attacked a British sentry. A small force of soldiers, under the leadership of Captain Preston, came to his aid, and seven soldiers shot dead five of the gang. The captain and the soldiers were put in jail, where they stayed for seven months until they were brought to trial. By this time, some of the hostility against the soldiers had died down. Adams proved that they had acted under extreme provocation. Captain Preston and most of the soldiers were discharged. The remaining two were found guilty of manslaughter and were branded on the hand.

to ally with the Americans against the British in the American Revolution. He achieved recognition of American independence and a loan from the Netherlands. From 1780 to 1782 he was sent to Britain to agree peace terms after the Revolution. He returned to Britain in 1785 as the first American ambassador to that country.

As delegate for Massachusetts to the First and Second Continental Congresses during the war with Britain, Adams argued strongly that the states should join together to form a confederation and fight for their independence. In 1776, he played a leading role

When Adams took up his post as a teacher at a school in Worcester, Massachusetts, he rode on horseback the sixty miles there from his home in one day.

Adams was a member of the committee which drafted the Declaration of Independence and submitted it to Congress for approval.

The signatories of the Declaration of Independence. The committee for the drafting of the document are featured in the foreground of this engraving celebrating the event. They were (from left to right) Philip Livingston, John Adams, Thomas Jefferson, Benjamin Franklin, Roger Sherman and, in the center, John Hancock.

Because he was short and stocky, and because he liked to be addressed with grand titles, Adams was nicknamed "His Rotundity" by some of his political opponents.

in persuading the Second Continental Congress to adopt the Declaration of Independence. Due to his efforts, Congress adopted the colonial army, and his strong and active support enabled George Washington to become its Commander-in-Chief.

Adams was also very involved in drafting and passing the Constitution, and he framed the constitution of his home state of Massachusetts.

Jefferson wrote, "To him more than any other man is the country indebted for its independence."

THE SIGNERS OF THE DECLARATION OF INDEPENDENCE

Because he founded the U.S. Navy, there
is always a USS John Adams.

Adams as a man

His ability to speak clearly and convincingly was useful to him as a lawyer and as a politician. His skill as an orator drew attention away from the fact that he was rather short, fat and bald.

Despite his talents and his achievements, he also had his faults. He was vain, jealous and short-tempered. He often imagined people were criticizing him unjustly and plotting against him. This is why Benjamin Franklin said, "John Adams is always an honest man, often a wise one, but sometimes and in some things absolutely out of his senses."

Adams knew his faults and tried to overcome them, writing when he was twenty years old, "Vanity, I am sensible, is my cardinal vice, and cardinal folly."

His Presidency

Adams was elected President in 1796, having served as Washington's Vice-President for his two terms in office. By this time, the power of the two political parties, the Democratic Republicans and the Federalists, had increased so that the election was fought on party lines. John Adams, the Federalist candidate, was elected by a majority of only three votes and Thomas Jefferson, the leader of the Democrats, became his Vice-President. In fact, this combination worked very well, and the two became lifelong friends who held each other in mutual

Adams was the first President to take up
residence in the White House. However, it was
not completed then, and his wife found it very
difficult and inconvenient.

respect. Although Adams was the Federalist candidate, Alexander Hamilton was the leader of the party, and Adams often had to contend with opposition from both sides.

In addition to party problems, Adams had to deal

The original White House, which was later to be burned by the British in 1812.

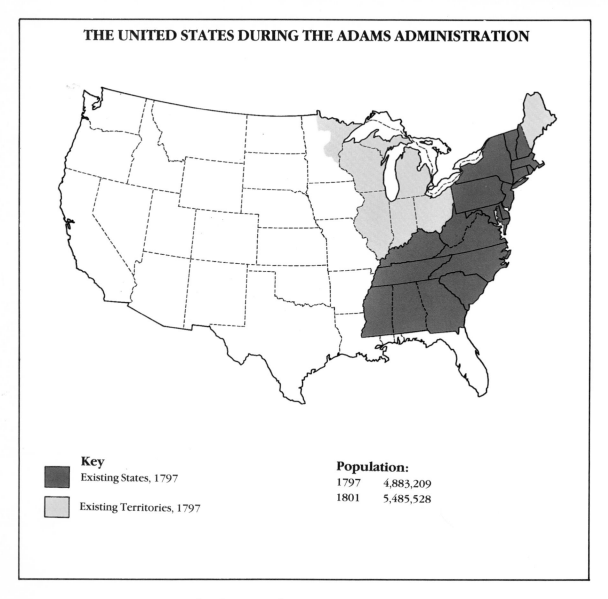

THE UNITED STATES DURING THE ADAMS ADMINISTRATION

Key
Existing States, 1797

Existing Territories, 1797

Population:
1797   4,883,209
1801   5,485,528

with the revolutionary government of France, which was harassing U.S. shipping and trade. When Adams sent negotiators to France, Talleyrand, the French foreign minister, demanded a bribe to prevent American merchant ships from being seized. When news of this outrage reached Congress, there were cries for war.

Adams persuaded Congress to establish a navy to protect American shipping. He realized that the United States could not afford to go to war. He feared its unity as a nation would be split along party lines. Acting on his own initiative, he re-opened negotiations with France. After eighteen months, agreement was reached, protecting American commerce and saving her from a needless war. Despite the anger of his own party over his actions, Adams regarded the fact that he kept the peace between the U.S. and France at this time as his greatest achievement.

His measures to deal with the growing calls for greater power for individual states and less for the federal government were less successful. In 1798, the Alien and Sedition Acts curbed the freedom of speech and of the press and gave the President the right to expel aliens. This caused Republicans such as Thomas Jefferson and James Madison to retaliate by attacking the right of the federal government to pass laws which were binding on individual states. In the vote for President in December 1800, Adams was defeated by Thomas Jefferson and Aaron Burr.

Later life

He retired to "Peacefields" near Quincy, with Abigail and their family, until his death — on July 4, 1826 — at the age of nearly ninety-one. He maintained an interest in public affairs and corresponded regularly with his friend Jefferson. Before he died, his eldest son, John Quincy Adams, became the sixth President of the United States, the country which he had done so much to establish.

BIOGRAPHY BOX

John Adams

Birthplace	Braintree (now Quincy), Massachusetts
Date of birth	October 30, 1735
Education	Harvard
Profession	Lawyer
Presidential term	March 4, 1797 to March 4, 1801
Party	Federalist
Place of death	Braintree (now Quincy), Massachusetts
Date of death	July 4, 1826
Place of burial	Braintree (now Quincy), Massachusetts

THOMAS JEFFERSON
(1743-1826)

Third President: 1801-1809

*Author of the Declaration of Independence
and father of the University of Virginia*

Thomas Jefferson lived through a period in history when the established order was being questioned. Across the western world, in places as far apart as France and North America, monarchies were being challenged and sometimes overthrown. Since time immemorial, countries had been ruled by kings and queens who had absolute power. Ordinary people had very few of the personal liberties which we take for granted today. They had to live and work where they were told by rich landowners on whose estates they happened to be born. They had to work, and work hard, for whatever wages the landowner decided to give them. Laws and punishments were harsh, and most people had no voice in the governing of their country.

Jefferson was an intelligent man with an enquiring mind. He read the books of the British and French philosophers of his time, who argued that individuals have basic rights which rulers must not be allowed to take away. He agreed with their ideas and was very involved in movements to increase the power and freedom of ordinary men, so that they had some control over their lives and over their government. He believed passionately in freedom.

President John F. Kennedy summed up the breadth and variety of Jefferson's knowledge, interests and talents when he said to a group of forty-nine Nobel prize winners attending a White House dinner, "I believe this is the most extraordinary collection of human talent, of human knowledge, that has ever been gathered together at the White House, with the possible exception of when Thomas Jefferson dined alone."

Nevertheless, Jefferson was still a man of his times. When he talked of the rights of the common man, he really meant men like him, wealthy and educated. He was not prepared to give power to all men. His definition of common man did not include those who were poor, uneducated, or landless. It did not cover native Indians or Negro slaves. He did, however, treat people humanely on a personal level, and his own slaves were well-treated and showed him love and respect. He believed that the slaves should be freed and sent back to Africa, but he was not prepared to fight against the overwhelming public opposition to their emancipation.

Family and education

Like George Washington, Thomas Jefferson was a Virginian. His father was a planter and surveyor of Welsh descent. He died when Thomas was fourteen, but not before he had instilled in his son the importance of learning and education. Thomas entered the College of William and Mary, the best center of learning in Virginia. After graduating, he became a successful lawyer, and his legal income, together with the profits from his estate of ten thousand acres and two hundred slaves, made him a wealthy man.

In 1772, he married Martha Skelton, a wealthy widow, and took her home to the beautiful house,

Jefferson designed
his home at
Monticello.

THE UNITED STATES DURING THE JEFFERSON ADMINISTRATION

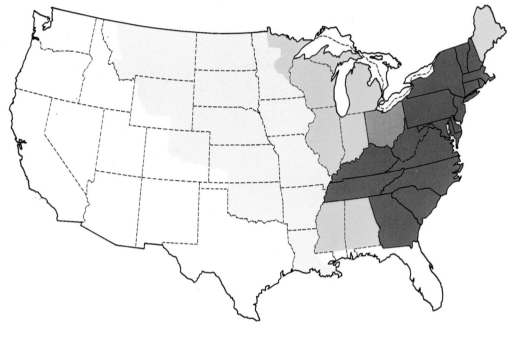

Key

 Existing States, 1801

 New States, 1801-09

 Existing Territories, 1801

New Territories, 1801-09

Population:

1801	5,485,528
1809	7,030,647

Monticello, which he was having built to his own design in Albemarle County. Architecture was one of his many and varied interests. They had five daughters and a son; sadly, only two daughters survived beyond infancy. When Mrs. Jefferson died ten years later, he grieved intensely and felt her loss bitterly. He devoted himself to his children, who loved him dearly.

Political career

He was elected to the Virginia House of Burgesses at the age of twenty-six. He was also appointed as Chief Commander of the King's militia in Albemarle County and became county surveyor. In 1773, he drafted the "Summary View of the Rights of British America" for the Virginia Convention. This document set out Jefferson's view that, as America was a new country, her citizens were not subject to the workings of the British Constitution and should be governed by laws passed by their own assemblies. The Convention, rejected the document, but it was published in London, where it was naturally disliked.

Jefferson attended the Second Continental Congress in Philadelphia in 1775, and a year later, he drafted the Declaration of Independence for which he is famous. It stated that the American colonies no longer regarded themselves as subject to Great Britain because Britain had violated American rights. Jefferson set out what he believed about individual freedom: "We hold these truths to be self-evident: that

Jefferson's design for the Presidential seal.

Jefferson invented the swivel chair, a revolving music stand and a mechanical device for bringing his clothes to him in his closet. He thought of the idea for automatic doors. He was the first American to be inoculated against smallpox and the first American to grow a tomato. It is thought that he introduced ice cream, waffles and macaroni into the United States.

45

The revolving chair was one of Jefferson's many inventions.

all men are created equal, that they are endowed by their Creator with certain unalienable Rights, that among these are Life, Liberty and the pursuit of Happiness."

During the American Revolution, he was a member of the Virginia House of Delegates and Governor of Virginia for two terms. He was the driving force

In addition to being a scholar of Greek and Latin and owning a wonderful collection of books, Jefferson had a practical turn of mind. He took a close interest in the farming of his estate and invented a plow which won a prize from the French National Institute of Agriculture. He experimented with the introduction of new crops and used methods to improve yields and make life easier for the farm laborers.

behind laws reforming the ownership and inheritance of land and establishing religious freedom in the state. One of his plantations was plundered by the British, and he himself only narrowly avoided being captured in his own home.

In 1784, he went as Minister to France, succeeding Benjamin Franklin. Although he reveled in the opportunity to study at first hand the artistic, scientific, culinary and architectural achievements of Europe, his time there confirmed his belief that a republic was a far better system of government than a monarchy. He visited England and met King George III. Jefferson was not impressed!

"My God!," he wrote, "how little do my countrymen know what precious blessings they are in possession of, and which no other people on earth enjoy. I confess I had no idea of it myself."

On his return, he was persuaded by George Washington to serve in his Cabinet as Secretary of State. This led to constant disagreements between Alexander Hamilton and Jefferson. Washington chose to have both of them in the Cabinet to try to bring together the two opposing political parties, the Federalists and Democratic Republicans. Hamilton was leader of the Federalists, who wanted a strong national government; Jefferson led the Democrats, with their emphasis on the rights of individuals and states. One major area of disagreement was fiscal policies and Hamilton's establishment of a National

Bank. Jefferson resigned in 1793, following a disagreement with Hamilton over America's role in the war between Great Britain and France. He returned to Monticello, where he continued to build up the Democratic Republican party. He was elected as John Adams' Vice-President in 1797.

The Presidency

Jefferson was elected President in 1800. He reduced the army from 4,000 to 2,500. Excise taxes were abolished, and those imprisoned under the Sedition Act of Adams' Presidency were freed. He made government economies by cutting the number of diplomats and reducing the size of the navy. The Judiciary Act was repealed. The navy was used to force the Barbary pirates to stop attacking American merchant ships and ransoming prisoners.

Louisiana was purchased in 1803 for fifteen million dollars from Napoleon, who was now First Consul of France. This deal gave the U.S. a piece of land bigger than the original thirteen states which had formed the new nation. It cost about eight cents an acre and consisted of all the territory now within the borders of Arkansas, Mississippi, Iowa, Oklahoma, Kansas, Nebraska and South Dakota, as well as large parts of what are now the states of Louisiana, Minnesota, North Dakota, Colorado, Wyoming and Montana.

The acquisition of such vast new territories increased Jefferson's popularity, and he was re-elected for a second term in 1804 with one hundred and sixty-two votes to only fourteen for C. C. Pinckney. The method of electing a vice-president was changed: instead of the runner-up to the presidency automatically becoming vice-president, separate elections were held for the post. This was done to prevent a repetition of Jefferson's first election as President. He had tied with Aaron Burr, and the House of Representatives had to choose between them. The Republican, George Clinton, was elected vice-president.

A continuing and serious problem during Jefferson's

The hot-tempered Aaron Burr killed Alexander Hamilton in a duel in 1804.

second term was the continual harassing of American shipping by Britain and France. Eventually, in 1807, an embargo prevented U.S. ships from sailing for foreign ports and restricted foreign vessels from taking cargoes out of U.S. ports. Jefferson imposed the ban in the hope that their loss of trade would force France and Britain to respect American rights to trade. He wanted at all costs to avoid war. In fact, the embargo hurt the United States more than it did France and Britain and led to great hardship and poverty.

After the Louisiana Purchase, Jefferson sent his secretary, Lewis, and William Clark with a party of thirty-four soldiers and ten civilians on an expedition to cross the continent and explore the new territory. Helped by Shoshone Indians, they reached the Pacific on November 7, 1805, having traveled through British Columbia.

Jefferson repealed the embargo a few days before the end of his second term.

His return to Monticello

Jefferson was happy to return to his beloved Monticello, but he remained interested and involved in political affairs. He corresponded frequently with his friends, and his advice was sought by Presidents Madison and Monroe who succeeded him. He advised President Monroe not to allow the United States to become embroiled in European wars over the sovereignty of South America.

The major task which Jefferson undertook during these years was the founding of the University of Virginia. He raised the money, designed the buildings and supervised their construction. He chose the academic staff, laid down the rules under which it was to be administered and selected the subjects which

The Louisiana Purchase, and the route taken by Lewis and Clark to reach the Pacific.

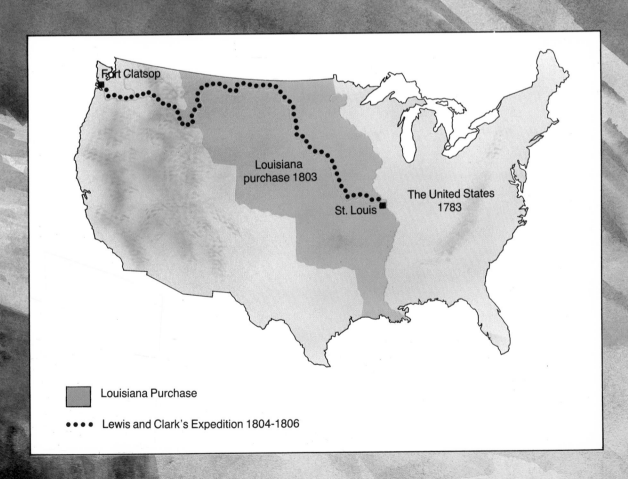

Fort Clatsop

Louisiana purchase 1803

St. Louis

The United States 1783

■ Louisiana Purchase

•••• Lewis and Clark's Expedition 1804-1806

were to be studied. He called it "the hobby of my old age."

Although Jefferson was a wealthy man, he was also generous and extravagant. By the time of his death, he was heavily in debt, and his estate and property had to be sold by his family. He lived in good health until 1826, when he was eighty-three. He died on the Fourth of July, the fiftieth anniversary of the signing of the Declaration of Independence and only a few hours earlier than his friend, former President John Adams.

Designing and founding the University of Virginia filled much of Jefferson's time after he retired from the Presidency.

BIOGRAPHY BOX

Thomas Jefferson

Birthplace	Shadwell, Virginia
Date of birth	April 13, 1743
Education	College of William and Mary
Profession	Lawyer
Presidential term	March 4, 1801 to March 4, 1809
Party	Democratic-Republican
Place of death	Monticello, Virginia
Date of death	July 4, 1826
Place of burial	Monticello, Virginia

JAMES MADISON
(1751-1836)

Fourth President: 1809-1817

Family and early life

Like Washington and Jefferson, James Madison was a wealthy Virginia planter and landowner. He was born in King George County in 1751, the eldest of ten children. His father was a farmer of English descent. James Madison graduated with degrees in history and government from the College of New Jersey, which is now Princeton University. He spent a further year studying Hebrew. Although he was physically small and unimpressive — Washington Irving described him as "but a withered little apple-john" — he had a fine mind. He suffered from ill health as a young man and expected to die at an early age; in fact, he lived until he was eighty-five.

In 1794, he married Dolley Payne Todd, a widow with one son. She was a popular and charming woman who enjoyed entertaining in the White House and on Madison's 2500 acre estate, Montpelier. As wife of the Secretary of State in the widower Thomas Jefferson's Cabinet, she often acted as hostess in the Jefferson White House, as well as during her husband's Presidency. She had a son from her first marriage, but the Madisons had no children together.

Dolley Madison was a popular and accomplished hostess at the White House for Presidents Jefferson and Madison.

> **Mr. and Mrs. Madison were very hospitable and enjoyed entertaining at their estate, Montpelier. Once they held a dinner on the lawn for ninety people.**

Political achievements

Madison was active in the political life of his home state as a member of the Virginia legislature. He had been a member of the committee which drafted a new constitution for Virginia in 1776. It was largely due to his efforts that religious freedom was written into the state's constitution. At twenty-nine, he was the youngest member of the Second Continental Congress from 1780-3.

On his return to Virginia, he studied law. When he was elected to the House of Delegates, he introduced Thomas Jefferson's bill to establish religious freedom in Virginia. His skillful management and persuasion helped that bill to become law. He was also instrumental in the decision to guarantee the free navigation of the Mississippi River. He was the Virginia delegate to the Convention of Philadelphia of 1787 and took an active role in the Convention's task of drawing up a constitution for the new United States. The confederation which the thirteen states had agreed during the American Revolution was proving ineffective as a permanent form of government. The aim of the Convention was to achieve a balance of power between the individual states and the federal

> **Madison Avenue, New York, is named after James Madison. This is rather ironic because today Madison Avenue is the center of the advertising industry, yet Madison the President was a quiet man who generally worked behind the scenes and did not promote himself.**

government. It was necessary for the United States to govern and negotiate as a country, and yet each state wanted to retain some degree of independence and self-government. The delegates decided that government must derive its authority from the people, but no section of the population should have too much power to dominate the rest.

After much debate, it was agreed that the number of places allocated to each state in the House of Representatives should be determined by the size of each state's population. A slave counted as three-fifths of a person for the purposes of representation and taxation. In the Senate, each state would elect two

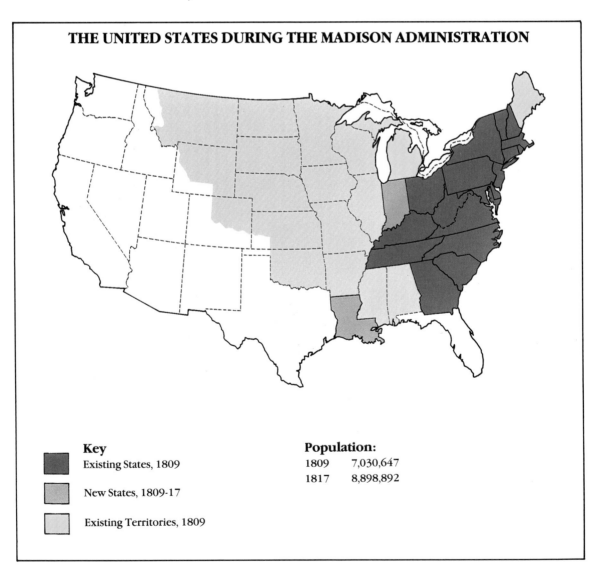

THE UNITED STATES DURING THE MADISON ADMINISTRATION

Key
Existing States, 1809

New States, 1809-17

Existing Territories, 1809

Population:
1809   7,030,647
1817   8,898,892

One of the causes of the War of 1812 was the British custom of *impressing* American sailors who claimed to be citizens of the United States. Impressment meant that the men were forced to serve on British ships against their will.

members, regardless of its size or population.

Madison, a firm opponent of slavery, disapproved of the compromise which postponed a decision on its abolition. This agreement made it illegal for Congress to ban trading in slaves before 1808.

The Constitution came into effect in 1789, and Madison continued to play an active part in politics. As a member of the House of Representatives, he proposed the first ten amendments to the Constitution, which formed the basis of the Bill of Rights.

In 1800, when his friend Thomas Jefferson was elected President, Madison was appointed as Secretary of State. They worked together harmoniously with varying degrees of success. The Louisiana Purchase, in which the United States bought a huge piece of land from Napoleonic France at a bargain price, was a popular achievement. Their policy of putting an embargo on American shipping trade in an attempt to force Britain and France to stop attacking U.S. vessels failed. It caused more hardship for Americans than for the aggressors and was abandoned. Nevertheless, Jefferson was so popular when he retired that Madison, his chosen successor, was elected President with a large majority.

Madison's Presidency

Despite his qualities of intelligence, diligence and attention to detail, Madison's two terms as President were not happy ones for him or the country. Foreign policy problems with Britain and France and their harassment of American shipping continued. Anger against Great Britain was aggravated by a suspicion that she was behind the increasing resistance of the Indians to white settlement of their lands. A confederation of tribes under the leadership of Tecumseh, a great Shawnee chief, achieved some success until they were defeated by General William Henry Harrison at the Battle of Tippecanoe in 1811. Problems with the Indians remained, however, because of the pressure of white frontiersmen pushing farther and farther west into Indian tribal lands. In 1812, Madison gave in to the public outcry and declared war against Britain shortly before his re-election to a second term.

"Mr. Madison's war"

The decision to declare war was a grave error. Madison's personality was not that of a successful war leader, and the nation was militarily and financially unprepared. Disaster and humiliation followed when the national capital at Washington, D.C., was seized by the British. Troops set fire to public buildings, including the White House itself, which escaped being totally destroyed only because of a downpour of rain. Despite this severe setback, the United States held on, and peace was eventually agreed at the Treaty of Ghent, signed on Christmas Eve, 1814. By its term, no territory was won or lost by either side as a result of the war. General Andrew Jackson was unaware of the peace treaty; fifteen days later, he won a famous victory at New Orleans.

Because no territory was lost and because of

BIOGRAPHY BOX

James Madison

Birthplace	Port Conway, Virginia
Date of birth	March 16, 1751
Education	College of New Jersey (later Princeton)
Profession	Lawyer
Presidential term	March 4, 1809 to March 4, 1817
Party	Democratic-Republican
Place of death	Montpelier, Virginia
Date of death	June 28, 1836
Place of burial	Montpelier, Virginia

Jackson's success, Madison began to regain popularity and was able to establish a second Bank of the United States in 1816. Relations between Britain and the U.S. improved with Britain's acceptance that there was no possibility of re-imposing colonial rule.

After the Presidency

Madison retired in 1817 and returned to Montpelier, where he enjoyed life as a country gentleman and entertained his many friends lavishly. He was president of the local Agricultural Society and took an active interest in the running of his estate, experimenting with crops and breeding stock. He succeeded Thomas Jefferson as rector of the University of Virginia, to which he bequeathed his fine library. The books, unfortunately, were destroyed in a fire in 1895. He was principally interested in books about government, natural history, science and new inventions. He edited papers on the Federal Convention of 1787. In his last years, he was crippled by rheumatism and lived in one room. He died at the age of eighty-five in 1836.

The U.S.S. Constitution routs the British during Mr. Madison's War.

GLOSSARY

agriculture — farming

alien — a person from a foreign country

ambassador — an official messenger sent by one government to another

cabinet — a small group of government officials who decide what the government should do

colonists — a group of people who settle in a new country, but who are still subjects of the government of their old country

confederation — a union, or joining together, of states

conscripts — people who are forced to join an army; the opposite of volunteers

constitution — the laws and agreements which give a government its powers

culinary — concerned with cooking

emancipation — setting free, especially from slavery or unjust laws

fiscal — concerned with taxation

free navigation — the right to sail without paying customs or tolls

impartial — not showing preference or favor

militia — a military force, usually made up of ordinary citizens in an emergency to reinforce the regular army

monarchs — kings and queens, who usually inherit the right to rule a country

natural history — the study of animals and plants

orator — a person who makes speeches

philosopher — a person who tries to discover inner knowledge and wisdom

republic — a form of government in which the people have the power to choose their leaders

surveyor — a person who measures land and draws maps and plans of it

violate — disregard or break the terms of an agreement

INDEX

Numbers in *italics* refer to illustrations.